for

Mum and Dad, brother Ben

and Alice

J.F.

First published 2007 by Walker Books Ltd, 87 Vauxhall Walk, London SE11 5HJ

2 4 6 8 10 9 7 5 3 1

This book has been typeset in Gill Sans

Printed in China

British Library Cataloguing in Publication Data: a catalogue record for this book is available from the British Library

ISBN 978-1-4063-0724-5

www.walkerbooks.co.uk

Say Hello

Jack & Michael Foreman

WALKER BOOKS
AND SUBSIDIARIES
LONDON • BOSTON • SYDNEY • AUCKLAND

Left out

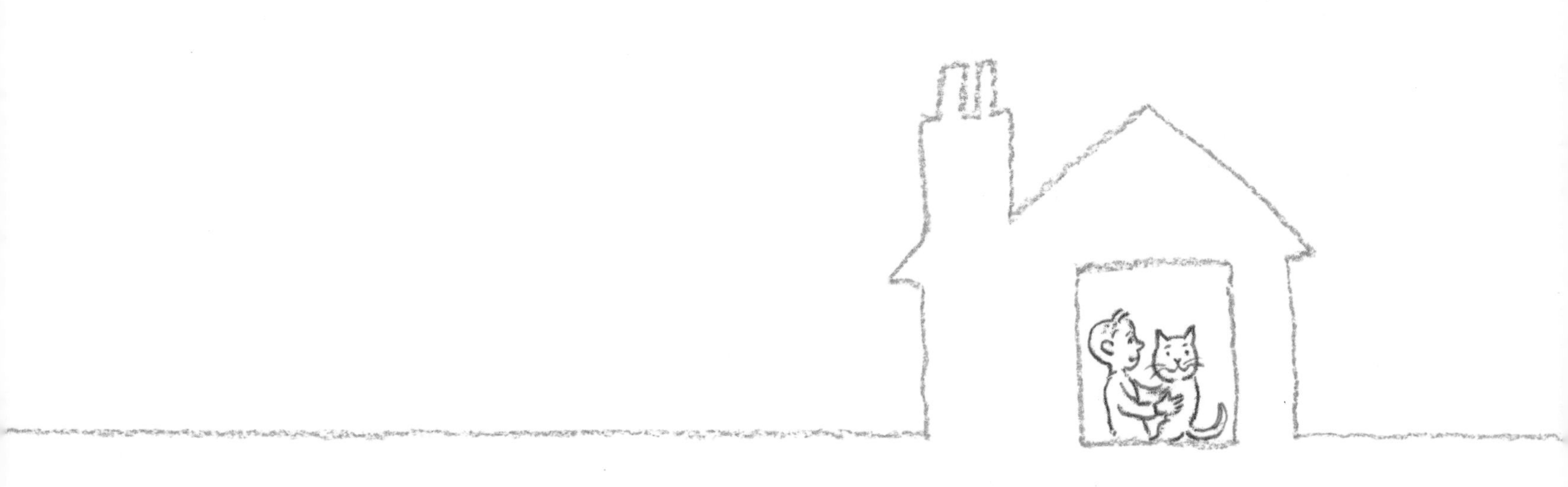

All alone

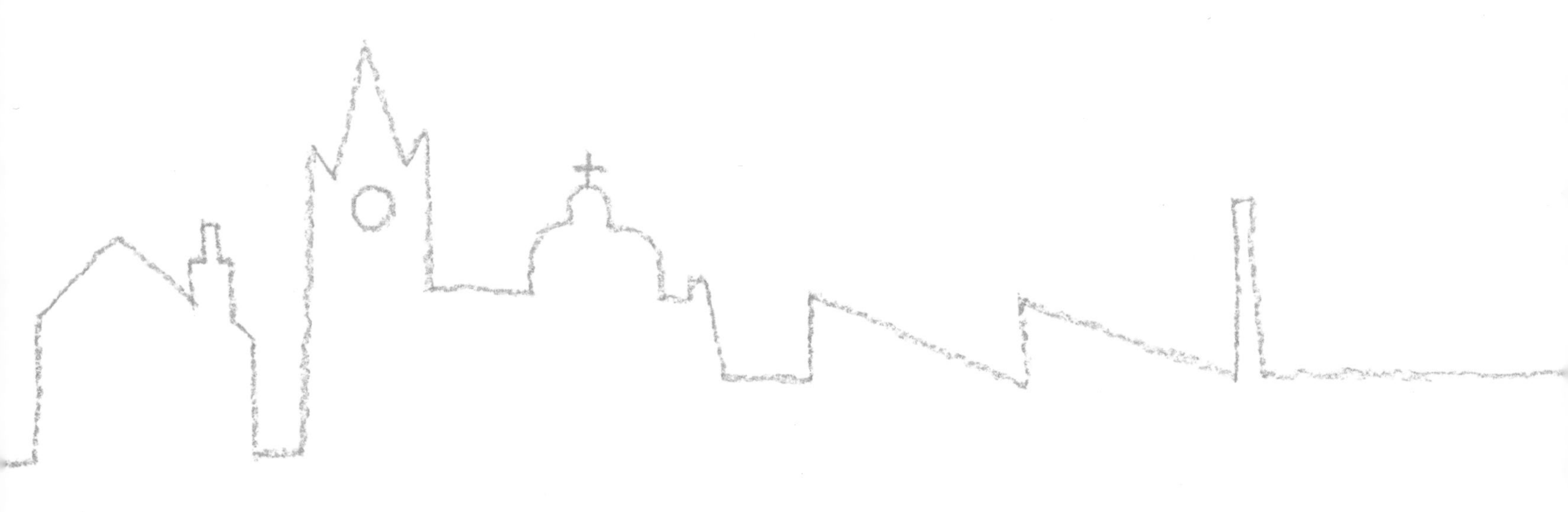

No friend, no home.

What's this?

Can I play too?

It’s great to make new friends like you!

Left out, no fun

Why am I the only one?

Left out, no fun

Why am I the lonely one?

Left out, no fun

I wouldn't do this

to anyone.

What's this?

Come and join the fun!

No need to be the lonely one.

When someone's feeling left out, low,

It doesn't take much to say …

Hello!

I Love this

Aloha! Shalom! Namaste!

Szia! Dia duit! Ciao!

Ave!

Konichiwa! Olá! Kia ora!

Sveiki!

Cześć!

Hellow! Labas! Hei! Sekoh!

Hola! Привет! 你好

Jambo! Salaam! Helô!